Sticker Dolly Dressing
Fashion Designer
Home Designer

Designed and illustrated by Stella Baggott

Additional illustrations by Antonia Miller

Written by Emily Bone

Contents

How to use this book

These pages will give you some hints and tips about using the stickers to create different designs for each room and how to decorate the book.

The stickers

If you look at the sticker pages you will see that some of the stickers are blank, some have patterns on them and some are fully colored.

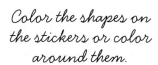 *Color in or draw patterns on the plain stickers.*

Color the shapes on the stickers or color around them.

 *Use small stickers like these to create your own patterns.*

Use the colored stickers just as they are.

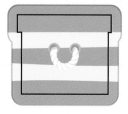

Warning!

The sticker paper is quite smooth, so if you are using felt-tip pens, leave the sticker for a little while before you peel it off. This will give the ink time to dry.

Designing a room

You can stick the stickers in any room in the book. They are arranged to match different themes, but you can mix and match them as much as you like. There are extra stickers too, to give you lots of choice for how you design each room.

Fill up empty shelves and blank walls or floors with your stickers. Think about which things will look good together.

Mood boards

Home designers make 'mood boards' to show where they got their ideas for colors, materials and themes. You'll find pictures and photos on some of the stickers. Use these to decorate the pages, once you have designed the room.

Ideas for colors to use on the stickers

Fill the empty space with stickers to make a mood board.

Ideas to try

Patterns, for wallpaper or material, are an important part of every room design. Below are examples of patterns you could draw on the plain stickers. There are more ideas later in the book, too.

There are more ideas later in the book, too.

Top Tip

It's a good idea to color in the stickers while they are still on the sticker pages, just in case you go over the edge of the shapes.

Samples of wallpaper or material like these are known as 'swatches'.

Nature lounge

Decorate this lounge with nature-inspired accessories, using bird, leaf and flower patterns. Use natural colors too – greens, blues, oranges and yellows.

Fill the space above with nature-themed swatches and photographs from the sticker page.

Here are ideas for colors to use in the room.

Flower bedroom

Home designers often use flower patterns to decorate rooms. Put the finishing touches to this colorful bedroom using a mix of big, bold flowers, and smaller, more delicate ones.

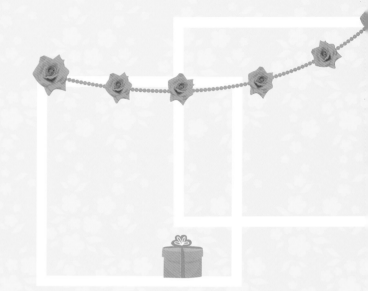

Stick flower pattern swatches here and color them in, using the colors on this page.

Design Ideas

Use a mix of pale and bright colors.

Folk wall

Folk art is a traditional style of design from northern Europe that uses simple shapes and bright colors. Fill these shelves and the wall with ornaments, vases and pictures inspired by folk art.

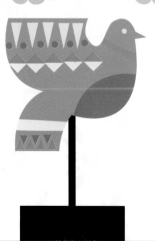

Stick the lampshade over this lightbulb.

Dressing room

Create a stylish dressing room using a mix of elegant furniture and accessories. There's a huge wardrobe to fill with clothes, shoes and boxes, too.

Patterned vases

Use the small stickers to decorate these vases with bold, colorful patterns. Add flower stickers to the ends of the stalks, too.

Colorful cushions

Adding patterned cushions to chairs, sofas and beds can create a striking look. Use the small stickers to add patterns and tassels to these cushions.

Retro kitchen

Some home designers look to the past for inspiration. This is called 'retro' design. This kitchen mixes modern styles with those inspired by the 1950s.

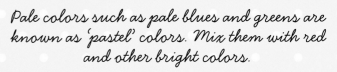

Pale colors such as pale blues and greens are known as 'pastel' colors. Mix them with red and other bright colors.

Fill this space with swatches,
objects and photographs
from the sticker page.

Design studio

Use the stickers to fill this room with everything you need for a fun, creative, yet super-organized studio for a fashion designer.

Adding design

Old furniture and accessories can be transformed into stylish, new things. Use the stickers to add your own designs to the things on these pages.

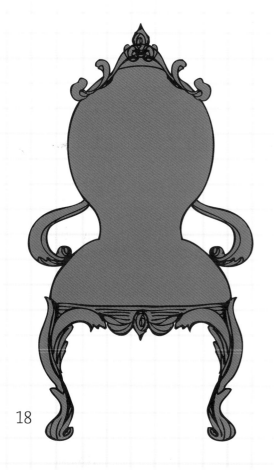

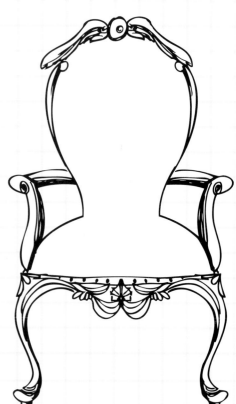

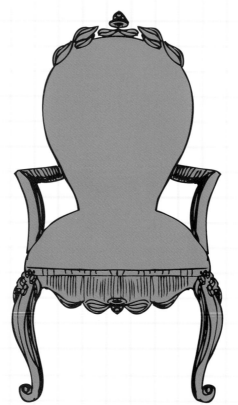

Color in the things on this page, as well as the stickers.

19

Relaxing garden

This calming garden is inspired by things you might find in a garden in China or Japan. Stick paper lanterns in the tree and add pots and plants to the ground.

Mix bright reds with soft greens, greys and blues.

21

Nautical den

'Nautical' is a design style inspired by boats and the sea. Use the stickers to create a den filled with shell, fish and boat patterns, and other things you might find by the sea.

Use blues and reds combined with sandy yellow and cream.

Fill the space above with nautical photographs and patterns from the sticker page.

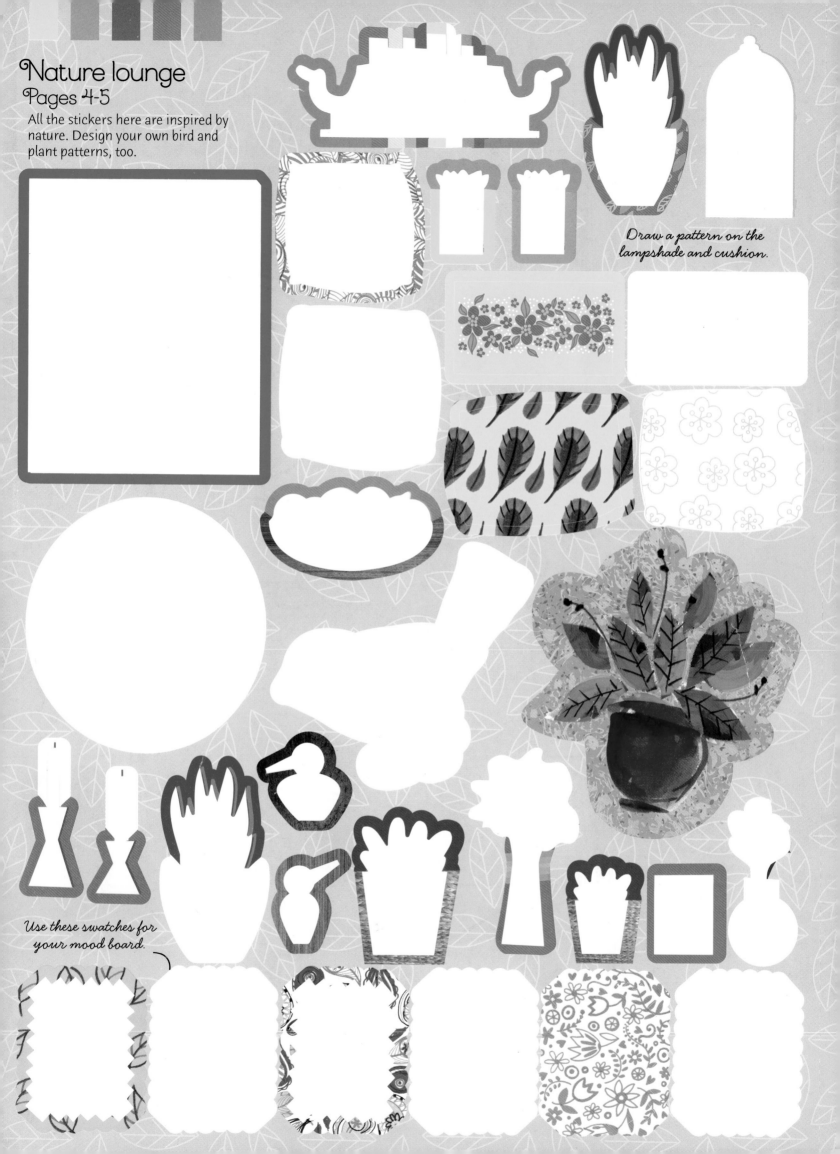

Nature lounge
Pages 4-5

All the stickers here are inspired by nature. Design your own bird and plant patterns, too.

Draw a pattern on the lampshade and cushion.

Use these swatches for your mood board.

Flower bedroom
Pages 6-7

Choose stickers to decorate the
bedroom, or decorate the blank stickers
with your own flowery patterns.

Color in these
swatches for
the mood
board.

Folk wall
Pages 8-9
Use these stickers to fill the shelves and wall with ornaments and pictures.

Draw your own folk art pictures in these frames.

Stick this lampshade over the lightbulb.

This picture was made by stitching patterns onto material. Design your own pattern, too.

Dressing room
Pages 10-11

Fill the dressing table, wardrobe and walls with the stickers on this page. The dresses can go on the dressmaker's dummy or on the hangers.

Sparkling chandelier light

Dressmaker's dummy

Stick these pictures on the wall. Design your own picture, too.

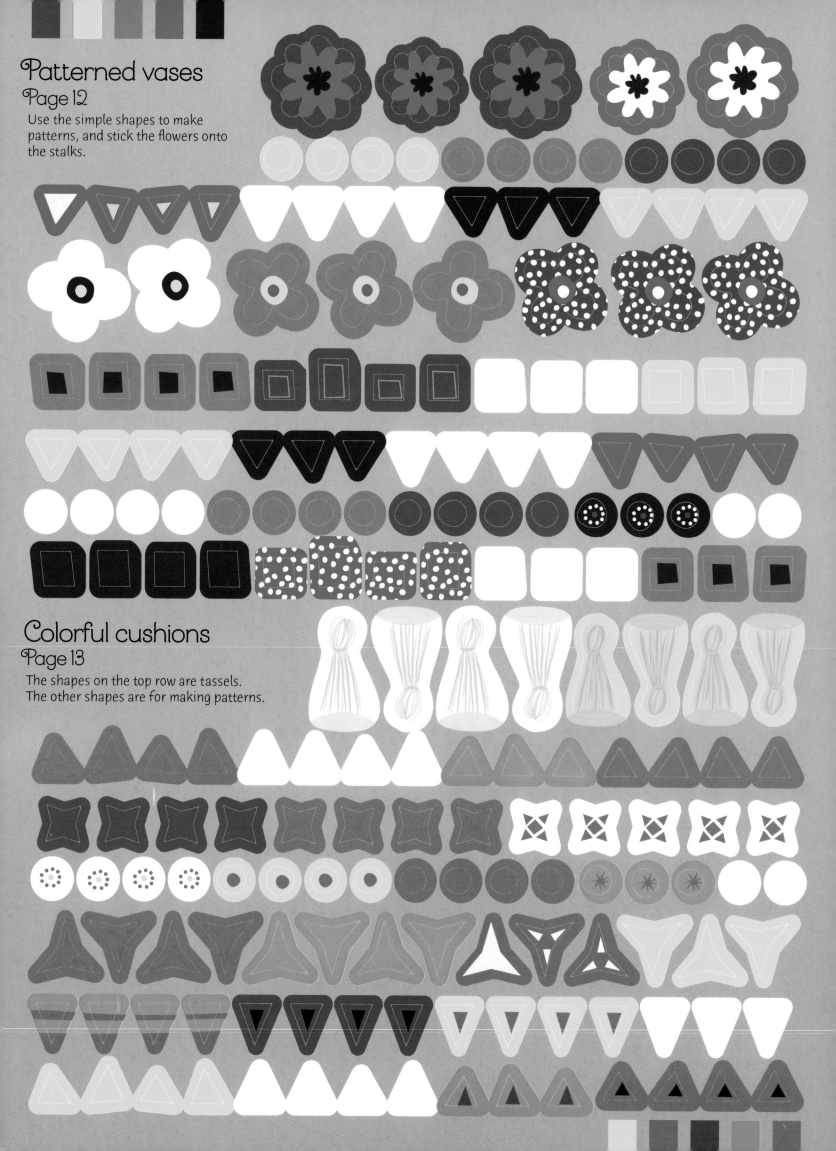

Patterned vases
Page 12
Use the simple shapes to make patterns, and stick the flowers onto the stalks.

Colorful cushions
Page 13
The shapes on the top row are tassels. The other shapes are for making patterns.

Retro kitchen
Pages 14-15

Use the stickers to fill your kitchen with these colorful, retro-inspired accessories.

Add these plates to the shelves.

Add these swatches to your mood board.

Design studio
Pages 16-17

Use the dressmaker's dummy to design your own dress. Dress the doll, too. Stick the other stickers on the shelves and desk.

Dressmaker's dummy

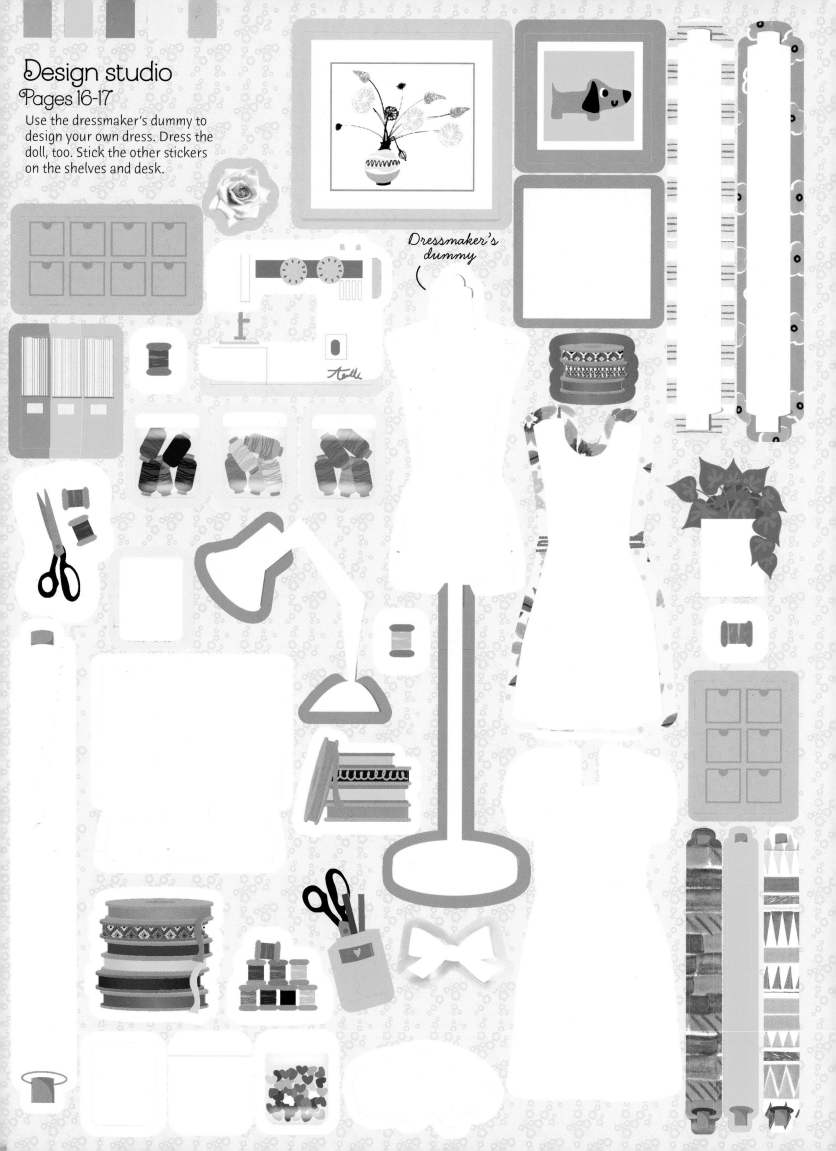

Adding design
Pages 18-19

Use the colored stickers as they are, or create your own designs on the blank stickers.

Stick these on the teacups.

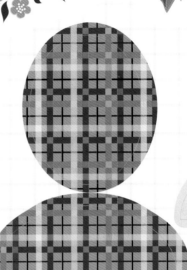

Use these to decorate the chairs.

Stick these on the clocks, or make your own.

Lampshades for the lamps

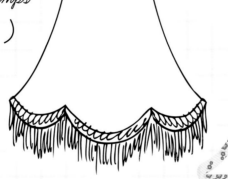

Put these pictures in the frames, or draw your own.

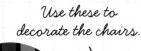

Relaxing garden
Pages 20-21
Use these stickers to create a peaceful garden.

Decorative lights

Color in the patterns on this cushion.

Pond

Paper lanterns

Bonsai tree
(a Japanese plant)

Nautical den
Pages 22-23

Add these stickers and design your own nautical patterns, too.

Add these things to the shelves.

Stick this driftwood coffee table in front of the sofa. Driftwood is wood that's been found on a beach.

Swatches for the mood board